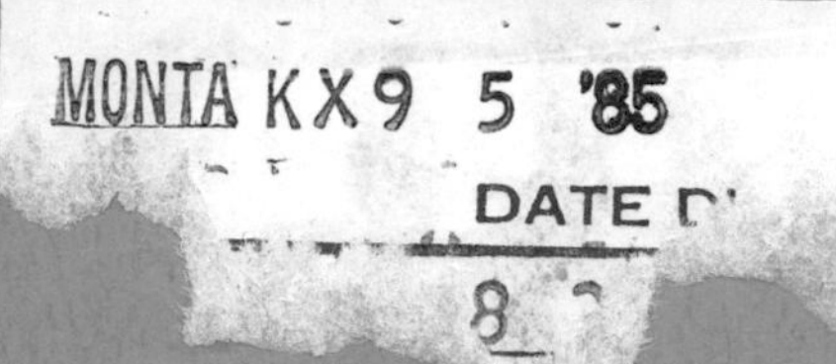
MONTA KX9 5 '85
DATE D
8

D0607471

#14533

THE WOMAN WITH THE EGGS

THE WOMAN WITH THE EGGS

BY HANS CHRISTIAN ANDERSEN

ADAPTED BY JAN WAHL · PICTURES BY RAY CRUZ

Crown Publishers, Inc. · New York

NOTE

The original version of *The Woman with the Eggs* is a poem written by Hans Christian Andersen when he was thirty years old. It was published December 17, 1836, in a weekly called *Den danske Bondeven*.

 Inquiries should be addressed to Crown Publishers, Inc., 419 Park Avenue South, New York, N.Y. 10016. Manufactured in the United States of America • Library of Congress Catalog Card Number: 74-77481 • Published simultaneously in Canada by General Publishing Company Limited • First Edition

The text of this book is set in 18 pt. Alphatype Bookman. The illustrations are pen and ink drawings reproduced in line with three additional flat colors pre-separated by the artist.

TO MY GJERTRUD
HELLO!

ONCE there was a woman who kept a hen.

Each day the hen laid a beautiful brown egg
that the woman put into a basket.

When she had a dozen big brown eggs
she decided to take them to market.
"I will sell them," she said, "and get
a whole dollar!"

Off she went with the basket on her head and

as she walked she talked to herself.

"With one dollar I can buy two more hens
and then—just think—I'll have three!
Three hens will start laying!

With eggs from three hens, why,
soon enough I can buy three more beauties!"

She sighed, seeing it all so clearly!
SIX HENS!

“Of the eggs they lay, I’ll sell off half.
The other half — I’ll hatch and then —

I'll have a true poultry farm.
Some will sit, some will lay!
Bless my soul, how clever I am!

And with my riches I'll buy a small sheep,

plus a gaggle of geese, and hand over
fist, how rich I'll be getting.

What with hens and eggs and

feathers and wool, I'll end
by having my money bags full!

I'll purchase a pig, I'll purchase a cow,
maybe even two, somehow.

I'll build me a barn,
I'll build me a sty!

And from the profits, I'll have

a fine house, servants, and
sheep grazing on the hill.

Now of course a handsome farmer
will come to woo me.
I'll have a husband and he'll have a missis.

He'll have a farm that is bigger than mine.

I'll be haughty and grand.
I'll be so superior!
And at everybody, I'll toss my head..."

And she did! She tossed her head!

SPLATT!

That proud silly woman who kept a hen!